To Justy;

On his 5th Birthday

With much love from his
" Bubie and Poppa "

February 2, 2002
Chatham, New Jersey

~ Justin Samuel Corbitt ~

WHAT PETE ATE

FROM

A - Z

where we
explore the English Alphabet
(in its entirety)
IN WHICH a CERTAIN DOG
DEVOURS
a MYRIAD of ITEMS which he
should NOT
by Maira Kalman

G.P. PuTNam's Sons

My name is Poppy Wise.

This is my little brother MOOKIE

and this is my dog PETE.

A good dog.
A VERY GOOD DOG.
But sometimes he is not
so good. He eats what he
should NOT. WHAT?
I will start with A.

All of it.

b   B   b

He ate a bouncing ball that belonged to uncle Bennie's dog Buster.

(Buster is no bargain. He barks all the time, but still...)

Bennie lived in a beautiful room that had a Bed, a Book, a Box, and a Bottle of water.

(And some other things that don't begin with B.)

He did NOT eat the cake from Olga, or the creamy cupcake. NO!

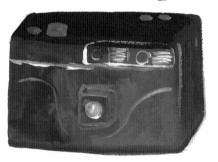

He ate my CAMERA!!
I LOVE to take pictures.
Look.

Baby Mookie
eating noodles.

My best friend
Doreen Parsley,
the great dancer.

d   D   d

He ripped the
head off my
dear doll Dinky.

Dreadful dog.

E

While Doreen and I
were making egg salad sandwiches
for the Egghead Club, Pete ran off with
EVERYTHING.

Egg slicer

Eggbeater

Egg Sandwich

Common cuckoo egg

Emu egg

Chinese Bulbul egg

Egads! Doesn't Pete know the difference between edible and inedible?

Edible	Inedible
apple	accordion
bread	ball
cake	camera
cupcake	doll
egg sandwich	eggbeater
honey	fez
ice pop	glue stick
jelly beans	homework
veal roast	money

f   F   f

He ate a FEZ.

FEZ is also a city in a country called MOROCCO in a continent called AFRICA.

(Not everyone in Fez wears a fez.)

G

While the Twinkle Twins were gluing together Mookie's Halloween costume, Pete GOBBLED the glue stick with Gusto.

GOOFY GLUEY DOG.

UHU GLUE

He ate half ($\frac{1}{2}$) of my homework. But did Mrs. Hoogenschmidt believe me? HA! (Hardly.) Horrible dog.

i   I   i

When I turned my back for an itsy iota of time, he ate my beautiful pink ice pop.

j   J   j

In a
jiffy
he ate 25
jelly beans   and he jumped for joy.

k k

He ate Mookie's magic KEY.

The Key opened Mookie's secret box. What's inside is a SECRET, but I will tell only You. (It is his KAZOO.)

At the Lucky Dog Show, he ate
all the leashes which let loose all

the dogs who ate all the lemon tarts and drank all the lemonade, and Mrs. Parsley was LIVID.

I don't want to make a
mountain out of a molehill,

Real (NO KIDDING) Money

But, he ate Bennie's money.

Holy Mackerel !

Buster says, "Nuts to Pete."

Now Bennie has no money (NONE) to buy Buster a new ball which, you will remember, Pete ate many letters ago.

n

N

n

H, once in a while we go into the woods and Pete is Perfect. Then I am of the opinion that this dog is O.K.

o   O   o

Oops, we are up to P p p

He ate Mrs. Parsley's pink pocketbook and she said, "Take that Pete back to the Pet Shop and get yourself a polite pooch."

Pooh on Mrs. Parsley.

q Q q

Quick Question.
Would you love a dog who ate your
lucky quarter, the Q from your
alphabet collection, your porcupine quill?
Even if for the quadrillionth time
you said, "Quit It.
Don't EAT that,"
and he Did, would
you still love that
dog?
Quite a lot.

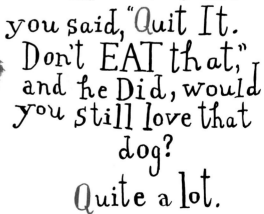

R R r

One Rainy day, he ate a rubber glove and the rubber band necklace Mrs. Parsley wore to a meeting of the Rubber Band Society.

Roberta Rothschild is the President of the Rubber Band Society.

Now Pete BOUNCES around the Room.

S

He ate Mookie's
stinky sneaker for
breakfast.
Doreen Parsley's
sandal for lunch.

s

Rocky's pointy shoe from Japan for dinner.

And a soft suede slipper for a midnight snack.

The Twinkle Twins have a dog named Twinky.
Twinky may look insane, but she
does not eAt theiR things.

u U u

You can understand that I would
be unhappy to say this, but Pete
ate cousin Rocky's underpants.
Uggh!

While Mookie was playing the violin (very badly thank you very much) Pete ran off with the veal roast.
VERY angry and hungry family.

w w W What can I say?

In his Wallet,
Rocky Keeps a
list of all the
times he was
insulted his
whole life.

It used to look
like this.

Who
What
When
Where
Why

Now it looks
like this.

WOW!

(Personally, I am happy Pete did it.)

y   Y   y

Yikes!

He ate

Mookie's   my   Doreen's
yo-yo,   yo-yo,   yo-yo

Now there will be NO YO-YO contest.

Oy - oy
oy - oy
oy - oy
oy - oy
OY.

and the yo-yos of the Twinkle Twins.

This is what he will not <u>not</u> eat.

ZUG ZUG DOG GRUB
(ZIP, ZILCH, ZERO.)

CAN YOU BLAME HIM?

PUBLISHED SIMULTANEOUSLY IN CANADA. PRINTED IN HONG KONG BY SOUTH CHINA PRINTING CO. (1988) LTD. DESIGN: JOLLY M&CO. PRODUCTION: MEAGHAN KOMBOL. THE ART WAS DONE IN GOUACHE. LIBRARY OF CONGRESS CATALOGING-IN-PUBLICATION DATA KALMAN, MAIRA. WHAT PETE ATE FROM A-Z / BY MAIRA KALMAN. P. CM. SUMMARY: IN THIS ALPHABET BOOK, A CHILD RELATES SOME OF THE UNUSUAL THINGS EATEN BY PETE THE DOG, INCLUDING AN ACCORDION, A LUCKY QUARTER, AND UNCLE NORMAN'S UNDERPANTS. [1. DOGS—FICTION. 2. ALPHABET.] I. TITLE. PZ7.K1256 WH 2001 [E]—DC21 2001019056 ISBN 0-399-23362-8 10 9 8 7 6 5 4 3 2 1 FIRST IMPRESSION

THIS BOOK IS FOR MY VERY BELOVED FAMILY (YOU KNOW WHO + WHERE YOU ARE) AND THE EXCELLENT DEAR BEAST HIMSELF. . . .